101 CHICKENS 1 FOX &
LOTS OF WEASELS

Author
D.A. Wysong

Illustrator
Anikina Irina

22 Muses Publishing

This book is dedicated to
Bobbi & Jesse,
and inspired by true events.

It all started when my brother and I began to itch. It was not just an ordinary itch. It was an itch that just would not quit. So, for about a day, my brother Jesse and I went around scratching ourselves constantly.

The next day, to our surprise, we woke up with little red spots all over our bodies. I looked at Jesse and Jesse looked at me. We then ran to tell our mom about our mysterious red spots.

We were immediately diagnosed as having the Chicken Pox. I was confused because I honestly could not remember the last time I had been around a chicken. I found out quickly that having Chicken Pox had nothing to do with a chicken besides the fact that we looked like a chicken whose feathers have all been plucked out.

Jesse and I had so many red spots that you could no longer see our skin. All you could see were red dot to dots. So, we began our quest. We started counting one another to see just how many red spots we had. For just a minute, I wanted to get a pen out and connecting the dots along Jesses' body. I never could pass up a good dot to dot. Why should I start now?

"Ninety-eight, Ninety-nine, One Hundred" I exclaimed as I finished the endless counting and searching for the magic number of his Chicken Pox spots. All I have to say is that there was a genuine satisfaction that came with finishing the task at hand. Now it was my turn to be counted.

Let me start by saying, Jesse is a rather good counter. Not as good as I am of course. You see I have had a little more classroom experience because I am an entire year older than him, but this was a real test. This was a firsthand project. His hands would be counting like it was on the job training. I was tempted to give him a pen to connect them. I was afraid of the number that he would produce. Not to mention, I was certain my mom just would not understand. So, we began. As Jesse got into counting, I thought that it would never end. It seemed to take forever for him to reach fifty. When he got to ninety, I was feeling pretty darn good. I knew it would not be much longer. He even managed to count the spots behind my ears. I was really impressed!

"Ninety-eight, ninety-nine, one hundred, one hundred and one" Jesse announced rather proudly. He was astonished that I had managed to have more spots than he did. Frankly, so was I as I looked over my arms and legs. We ran into the other room to make our announcement to our mom. I could tell she was quite unhappy as she looked us over front to back.

I will have to admit that now I was starting to get really kind of nervous. I overheard Mom telling Grandma that we might not be making it to see her for Christmas because we were contagious. Gee! What a thing to be for Christmas, CONTAGIOUS! What were we going to do? We had to think of something fast. We were really a spotted mess.

The snow was falling like a white blanket outside our window. The tree was twinkling with its dazzling lights. The smell of Christmas was flowing freshly. The songs of good cheer and joy filled our house each day. Yes, Christmas was definitely in the air. There was also the two of us, looking like Christmas geese, waiting for the big day. The question was would we be well enough to attend the family gathering of all our loved ones? We had to do something, anything.

Mom said it helps if you do not scratch. So, we wore mittens. It was hard to look out the window and see everyone having fun in the snow. Snowball fights, snowmen and snow forts being built in every yard but ours. The hardest part was watching everyone going down the hills in front of our house on their sleds. We were missing all of the fun!

I looked down at my mittens. I wished I could pack a great big snowball. Mom did let us make snowballs with vanilla flavoring on them. Another good thing was, at least we had cool mittens. Jesse was not scratching with the help of bugs and I with polka-dots. At least we had not lost our style.

We were also told to soak in a vinegar bath for at least a half hour. It keeps you from scratching, but it really stinks so I just hold my nose. Jesse does the same. It is really not too bad; the tub is big and had six jets. The water whirls and the bubbles are bubbling. The stinky bath is really working, and the mittens are not so bad.

Then it happened, I went to the bathroom and was minding my own business. Wouldn't you know it? I found five more chicken pox in a place where the sun does not shine, if you know what I mean! Of course, being the honest person that I am, I announced to the world, "I now have one hundred and six chicken poxes!" Mom really loved hearing that, but I wonder if Grandma knows.

As the days passed, I did get used to wearing the mittens all day and night. After a while, we did not need them anymore. It had been a week and we had just realized the school party was coming up in a few days. Christmas was just around the corner.

The long soaks were working. The crème we were anointed with each night seemed to being doing the trick. We were really scabbing up which is a good thing when you have the chicken pox. Boy, they were itching!

Jesse's began to fall off first. Good for him. He was almost in the clear. Just three more days until Christmas, what should I do? I was hanging in there, and mine were doing okay but they were also in plain sight for everyone to see. Even our dog seemed to turn the other way when I came in. Did I really look that bad?

As I thought about the days that had gone by, it put twelve days into a whole new light. We were counting the days all right. We were counting to see if we would have Christmas at all.

Of course, we would have Christmas, just on a smaller scale. We would not get to see Grandma and Grandpa. We would not get to see our favorite Aunt and Uncle. And then there was our uncle Shawn. He was really cool. He would always show us the latest in Karate moves. Not to mention all of our cousins who we rarely saw at all. And finally, Aunt Harriet well, you get the picture. I just could not bear to miss all of the fun and all of the food. Let us not forget the presents! Now we all know, as our parents have told us, getting presents is not the most important thing about Christmas, and I have to agree, but may I add that it is the most fun part of Christmas, YES!

So here we are, the night before the Christmas party at school. I really wanted to go. Heck, it was not fun to miss the fun at school. We always had to do the work and I certainly did not want to miss all of the fun and games of a party.

Just when we were least expecting it, Mom announced we were going shopping. This was a PARTICULARLY good sign. I can still remember those magic words Mom said, "You are going to be fine for Christmas." Ah, life is so wonderful.

Going out into the real world was a little strange after being inside for days on end. You kind of get used to how spotty you actually are. Let me tell you, you really get some looks. You really are a sore sight in the end.

We picked up some great presents and finished the shopping. We were heading home to get a good nights' sleep. We needed to rest up for the big day. We were, just imagine, thinking about going to school and having fun.

Overall, chicken pox was not too bad. Eventually we all experience some form of it. I am glad that mine is over. I am also glad that I had my brother to go through it with. The best part was that we were going to be able spend Christmas with the whole family.

My Mom was laughing, I thought she was going to lose it, Jesse asked if we had ever had the weasels. She thought that was really funny. I do think that he meant to say the measles. If you think about it though, having the weasels could be a genuine experience. Can you just imagine waking up with weasels hanging all over you? What a time that would be! One thing is for sure, they would be hard to count. So, for now I have to go, ah yes, and before I forget, Merry Christmas!

Author

D.A. Wysong is the Author of twenty six children's books including her series Creeper Ceepers based on myths & urban legends. Her new series Monster Hunters Of America will be available in 2023. Her latest book Ghosts of Northern Kentucky will be available September 2022. Her favorite genre is the paranormal.

The Illustrator

Anikina Irina, also known as Annibell, resides near middle Russia in the beautiful Ural Mountains. She especially loves to illustrate children's books and make the stories come to life. She enjoys working with watercolor and different pencil techniques.

Creeper Ceepers

A series of creepy scary stories for kids of all ages:

Series One

Book **One** – The Haunting of Grey Cliff Manor

Book **Two** – The Tale of the Greenwich Werewolf

Book **Three** – The Doll Maker

Book **Four** – Trilogy of Terror – Night of the Scarecrow, The Black-Eyed Kids & the Haunted Pumpkin Patch

Book **Five** – Trilogy of Haunted Yuletide Tales

Book **Six** – The Creepiest Cemetery Ever

Book **Seven** – Dark Sisters of the Craft

Series Two

Book **Eight** – The Haunted Road Trip

Book **Nine** – Soul Suckers & the Anatomy of a Cell Phone

Book **Ten** – Wendigos in the Woods

Book **Eleven** – Just One Shot

Book **Twelve** – Killer Clowns & the Crazed You-Tuber

Book **Thirteen** – Vampire Darkness in the French Quarter

Book **Fourteen** – Time Travel & The Knights Templar

Other Books by D.A. Wysong

Before Time Was

Tippy, Torry & the Mouse

A Nishy Pop Tale

A Rainy-Day Birthday

101 Chicken Pox & Lots of Weasels

So, You Want a Baby Alligator & Lots of Other Animals

Holding Zaylei

You Can Call Me Pickle Puss

The Song of Kenzie Bear

Shaun Lee's Super-Duper Trip to the Zoo

Scuba Diving with Kayden

Astrology 101- A Child's Guide to the Stars and Planets

Monster Hunters of America

COMING 2023

Printed in Great Britain
by Amazon

44098392R00016